Keep on Swinging!

A PRICE STERN SLOAN READER

By Tracey West
Based on a story by Howard Jonas

PSS!
PRICE STERN SLOAN

W9-BTB-731

PRICE STERN SLOAN
Published by the Penguin Group
Penguin Group (USA) Inc., 375 Hudson Street, New York, New York 10014, U.S.A.
Penguin Group (Canada), 90 Eglinton Avenue East, Suite 700, Toronto, Ontario, Canada M4P 2Y3
(a division of Pearson Penguin Canada Inc.)
Penguin Books Ltd, 80 Strand, London WC2R 0RL, England
Penguin Ireland, 25 St Stephen's Green, Dublin 2, Ireland
(a division of Penguin Books Ltd)
Penguin Group (Australia), 250 Camberwell Road, Camberwell, Victoria 3124, Australia
(a division of Pearson Australia Group Pty Ltd)
Penguin Books India Pvt Ltd, 11 Community Centre, Panchsheel Park, New Delhi - 110 017, India
Penguin Group (NZ), Cnr Airborne and Rosedale Roads, Albany, Auckland 1310, New Zealand
(a division of Pearson New Zealand Ltd)
Penguin Books (South Africa) (Pty) Ltd, 24 Sturdee Avenue, Rosebank, Johannesburg 2196, South Africa

Penguin Books Ltd, Registered Offices:
80 Strand, London WC2R 0RL, England

The scanning, uploading, and distribution of this book via the Internet or via any other means
without the permission of the publisher is illegal and punishable by law. Please purchase only authorized
electronic editions, and do not participate in or encourage electronic piracy of copyrighted materials.
Your support of the author's rights is appreciated.

© 2006 IDT Entertainment, Inc.
Used under license by Penguin Young Readers Group. Published in partnership with and licensed by
Major League Baseball Properties, Inc. The Major League Club insignias depicted in this product are
trademarks which are the exclusive property of the respective Major League Baseball Clubs and may not be
reproduced without their written consent. All rights reserved. Published by Price Stern Sloan,
a division of Penguin Young Readers Group, 345 Hudson Street, New York, New York 10014. PSS! is a
registered trademark of Penguin Group (USA) Inc. Printed in the U.S.A.

Library of Congress Cataloging-in-Publication Data

West, Tracey, 1965–
Everyone's hero : keep on swinging! / by Tracey West.
p. cm.
Summary: Yankee Irving loves baseball—especially Babe Ruth—so when Babe's bat is stolen,
Yankee enlists the aid of a talking baseball to go after the thief.
ISBN 0-8431-2119-X (pbk.)
[1. Baseball—Fiction. 2. Ruth, Babe, 1895–1948—Fiction.] I. Title.
PZ7.W51937Ev 2006
[E]—dc22
2006012080
10 9 8 7 6 5 4 3 2 1

Chapter 1

In 1932 Babe Ruth was everyone's hero. With his mighty bat, Darlin', Babe hit home run after home run. Thanks to Babe, the New York Yankees were winning the World Series. They were leading the Chicago Cubs 3-0.

Kids everywhere wished they could bat like Babe. Especially one kid in particular: a boy named Yankee Irving.

Yankee thought Babe was the best. Certainly, Babe was much better than Yankee himself. Every afternoon Yankee played baseball with the neighborhood

 boys in the sandlot. Yankee always got picked last, but he didn't care.

When it was Yankee's turn at bat, the other boys teased him.

"Don't swing, Irving!"

"Just take the pitch!"

But Yankee swung at every pitch, no matter how high or low it was. He missed once . . . twice . . . three times. Yankee was out!

"You're never playing on my team again!" one of the kids said angrily.

Yankee felt bad. He picked up a broom handle and a rock from the ground. He hit the rock like it was a baseball.

Smash! The rock broke the windshield of an old car. Yankee ran to the car. Underneath, he spotted an old baseball.

Yankee picked up the tattered ball.

"Guess nobody wants you in the game, either," Yankee said sadly. He stuffed the ball into his hat and walked home.

Pictures of baseball players covered the wall of Yankee's bedroom. Yankee suddenly didn't feel like looking at them anymore. He began to tear them off of the walls.

Then Yankee heard a thump. He turned around and saw the baseball rolling toward the door.

Yankee bent down to pick it up—and saw two blue eyes staring at him.

"How's it goin'?" asked the baseball.

"*Aaaaaah!*" Yankee screamed. The baseball was alive!

Chapter 2

Yankee didn't believe it at first, but the ball kept talking.

"I just gotta get out of here," said the ball. "I'm going back to the sandlot."

Yankee picked up the ball.

"Hey, watch it there, grabby hands!" the ball cried. "Don't make me go all Crazy Eight Ball on you."

Yankee wasn't about to let a talking baseball get away. He decided to name the ball Screwie. He showed Screwie to his mother.

"Mom, look. A talking baseball!" Yankee said.

Yankee's mom thought he was joking. She couldn't hear Screwie talk. Only Yankee could hear him.

Yankee gave Screwie a good cleaning in the sink. Then he stuck Screwie inside his underwear drawer. Yankee had an important errand to run.

Yankee brought dinner to his dad. Mr. Irving worked nights as a janitor at Yankee Stadium. Yankee loved being inside the empty stadium. It always felt like magic.

Yankee told his dad about striking out at the sandlot.

"I don't think I want to play baseball anymore," Yankee said.

Yankee's dad knew a way to cheer him up. He took Yankee to the Yankees locker room. Yankee stared in wonder at the jerseys and caps of the players. Then he came to Babe Ruth's locker. His bat, Darlin', gleamed in the darkness.

Yankee's dad left him alone in the locker room for a while. Then a strange-looking security guard came in. Yankee quickly left.

The next morning at home, Yankee talked to Screwie.

"Maybe you could give me some pointers about baseball," Yankee said. "I mean, you *are* one, right?"

"Kid, look. Baseball is only gonna break your heart," Screwie replied. "Trust me, I was in the Majors."

"You were in the Majors?" Yankee asked.

"I was in the Majors for two glorious pitches," Screwie said. "Tragically for me, I was a foul ball. Nobody even came to look for me."

A knock on the door got Yankee's

attention. It was Mr. Robinson, the owner of the Yankees. He told Yankee's dad that somebody had stolen Darlin' from the Yankees locker room!

Chapter 3

Yankee ran right out of his room. "There was a security guard in the locker room last night!"

Mr. Robinson was upset that Yankee's dad had left Yankee alone in the locker room.

"I have no other choice," he told Mr. Irving. "You're fired!"

Yankee felt terrible. His dad had lost his

job, and it was all his fault. But maybe he could help. That security guard had looked familiar to him.

Yankee ran into his room and looked through his baseball cards. Then he found the face he was looking for. He showed Screwie.

"It's Lefty Maginnis of the Chicago Cubs," Yankee said. "That's the security guard I saw last night."

"Lefty's the biggest cheater who ever

stepped on a pitching mound," Screwie said. "Hmm. The Yankees are clobbering the Cubs in the Series."

"Lefty stole the bat so Babe can't hit!" Yankee guessed. "The Yankees will lose the Series. If I could only find Lefty, I could get Darlin' back."

"You're just a kid," Screwie said. "You'll never find him. He's probably on a train to Chicago by now."

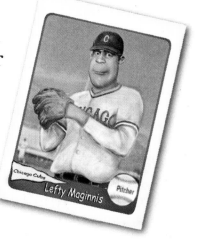

"Then if we go to Penn Station, we might catch him!" Yankee said.

Yankee grabbed Screwie and climbed out the window. He took the subway to Penn Station. He pushed his way through the crowd—and saw Lefty, carrying a long case.

"That's gotta be Babe's bat!" Yankee cried.

Yankee ran to a pay phone and called home.

"Mom, I'm in Penn Station. I think I found Babe's bat. Lefty Maginnis from the Chicago Cubs has it," Yankee said.

In the background the station announcer's voice blared: "Last call for Chicago! All aboard!"

Yankee panicked. He couldn't let Lefty get away. He hung up the phone and ran for the train. He climbed on board.

Chapter 4

Yankee walked the aisles looking for Lefty. He rolled Screwie under the seats to get a quick look. Screwie spotted Lefty, and Yankee took the bat from under his seat.

The train lurched as it started to leave the station. Yankee ran to the back of the train, but Lefty spotted him. Yankee had to get off that train!

There was only one thing Yankee could do. He took a deep breath and made a daring leap onto another train passing by. He made it!

Yankee had to get back to the platform. He looked behind him. Lefty jumped onto the train after him.

Yankee had to jump again—onto

another train passing by! Lefty jumped after him.

Yankee hid quietly in a train car. He could hear Lefty following him. Slowly and carefully, Yankee made his way to the back of the train.

Lefty caught up to him. Yankee was cornered. He had to make one more jump.

"*Oof!*" Yankee cried. He landed on the railing of the train headed for Chicago.

"Hang on, Yankee!" Screwie yelled.

Yankee felt the rail slipping from under his fingers. Lefty reached out from the other train, grabbing him and shaking him. Yankee struggled to climb into the car. The train tracks raced underneath him. His stomach flip-flopped. He was going to fall . . .

Smack! A train signal knocked Lefty to

his knees. Yankee scrambled into the train car. He was safe from Lefty—for now.

Yankee didn't get very far on the train. The conductor threw him off in Pennsylvania because he didn't have a train ticket.

Yankee wanted to get Darlin' back to New York, but the ticket booth was closed. He slumped against the wall of the train station. Then he opened up Darlin's case. He carefully lifted up the bat.

"Help! Help! Put me down!" she screamed.

Yankee stared at the bat in shock. Darlin' was alive!

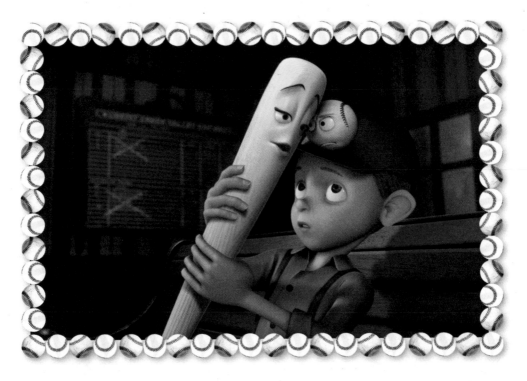

Chapter 5

"No! Wait! We're rescuing you," he tried to explain.

Darlin' didn't want anything to do with Yankee and Screwie. She tried to roll away. But she could only roll in a circle.

"I am not rolling all the way to Chicago," Darlin' said. "Pick me up and take me to Babe!"

"I can't," Yankee said. "When Lefty stole you, my dad got fired. If I take you to New York, then he'll get his job back."

Then Yankee saw a shadow outside the train station. It was Lefty!

Yankee hurried away before Lefty could spot him. He walked through the woods, not sure where he was going. Suddenly, a dog ran up. It snatched Screwie in its mouth and ran off!

Yankee chased the dog to an old factory. He met some men who were down on their luck. They were listening to the radio—and it was bad news.

"Babe Ruth is at the plate, and it's strike three!" the radio announcer cried. "The Cubs have won this World Series game."

"Babe needs me!" Darlin' said.

Yankee knew what he had to do. The next World Series game was being played in Chicago. "Babe is everyone's hero," he said. "And I can't let them down. We're going to Chicago!"

Yankee walked along the railroad tracks toward Chicago. He didn't know if he'd make it in time, but he had to try.

Soon Yankee was tired and hungry. He stopped at an apple orchard to pick some apples and put Screwie on the ground. Two boys came up. One of them, Tubby, picked up Screwie.

"Hey, put me down!" Screwie cried.

Yankee faced the boys. "Hey, give him back!"

Tubby threw Screwie to the other boy, Arnold. The bullies tossed Screwie back and forth.

"Ha-ha! Keep away!" Tubby yelled.

Yankee tried, but he couldn't catch Screwie. Suddenly, a bunch of apples flew through the air. Yankee turned and saw a girl throwing apples at the boys.

"You give him back that ball!" she yelled.

The bullies started throwing apples back. *Whack! Whack! Whack!* Yankee kept getting hit by the boys' apples.

"Aren't you going to dodge any of them?" the girl, Marti, asked.

"I'm trying!" Yankee cried.

"No you're not," Marti said. "Don't look where they're going. You've got to watch where they're coming from. Keep your eye on the apple."

Yankee followed Marti's advice. Soon he was able to dodge the apples coming at him. He threw more apples at Tubby and Arnold. The bullies gave up and ran off. Yankee happily picked up Screwie.

"Thanks," Yankee told Marti. "How did you learn to throw like that?"

"My daddy taught me how to pitch," she explained. "His name is Lonnie Brewster. He plays for the Cincinnati Tigers."

Marti took Yankee back to her house. She showed him pictures of her father's team. Yankee told her that he was trying to get Darlin' to Chicago so Babe could win the Series for the Yankees.

"My dad's team is going on the road tomorrow," Marti said. "They can drop you off in Chicago."

Yankee felt hopeful. They just might get to Chicago in time to help Babe.

Chapter 6

What Yankee didn't know was that while Marti and Yankee talked, Marti's mom called the police. She was worried that Yankee might have run away from home. But she didn't know about Lefty.

Lefty showed up at the Brewster house. He pretended to be Yankee's dad. Luckily, Yankee saw him coming. He took Darlin' and Screwie and ran away.

Lefty caught up to them.

"Give me that bat!" he cried.

"No!" Yankee said firmly. "I'm taking her to Chicago and giving her to Babe."

"You tell him, Yank!" Screwie cheered.

Whack! Whack! Whack! Marti threw apples at Lefty. He fell down, and Yankee got away.

Yankee walked and walked. He finally reached the Tigers' ball field. He found Marti's dad. Mr. Brewster said Yankee could ride on the Tigers' bus.

The Cincinnati Tigers thought Darlin' was a beautiful bat. They showed Yankee how to hold her

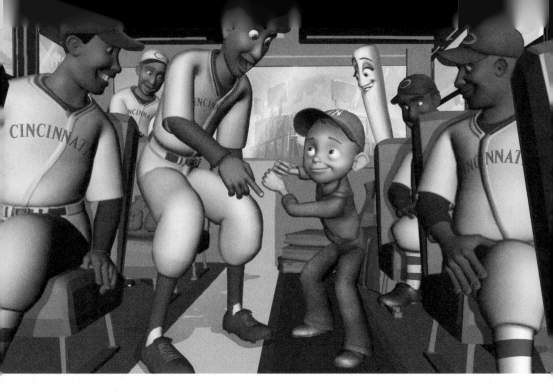

and how to stand when he was waiting for a pitch. It wasn't easy. The bus swayed back and forth. But Yankee held steady.

"Keep your knees bent," Mr. Brewster coached. "Spread your knees a little farther apart. That's it!"

The Tigers liked Screwie, too. They picked him up and tossed him around. One player threw Screwie out an open window, and another player caught him!

"*Whooo!* I don't like heights!" Screwie

wailed. Then he started to have fun.

"This is amazing! I'm a knuckleball!" Screwie cheered.

The Tigers dropped off Yankee at Babe's hotel in Chicago. The first thing Yankee saw when he stepped off the bus was bad news.

"Cubs Clobber Yankees," the newspaper headline read. *"Series Tied 3-3."*

Chapter 7

"They lost again today. We have to get to Babe!" Yankee said.

Just then, a fancy car pulled up in front of the hotel. A big man with a big smile stepped out.

"It's Babe!" Yankee cried.

A crowd of fans swarmed around Babe. Yankee could not get near him. Babe waved and smiled to everyone. Then he went inside the hotel.

Yankee ran after him. Babe walked into the dining room. Yankee tried to follow, but the maître d' stopped him.

"Take your soil, and yourself, out of my ballroom, please," he said.

"I need to talk to Babe!" Yankee said.

The maître d' chased after him. Babe thought the whole scene was funny.

"Hey, Mister D, bring that kid over here!" he called out.

Yankee finally stood face-to-face with Babe.

"I like your style, kid," Babe said. "You play baseball?"

"Uh, sure," Yankee said. "But I'm not such a good hitter."

"Keep swinging," Babe said. "That's the only advice I can give you."

Yankee suddenly remembered why he had come all the way to Chicago.

"Babe, I have your bat. I have Darlin'," Yankee said.

Yankee opened his backpack—but Darlin' was not in it!

"She was right here!" Yankee wailed.

"Sure, kid," Babe said. "You had a good story going, but you gotta work on the punch line."

Then Yankee saw Lefty slip out of the ballroom. He had Darlin'!

"Hey! Stop him!" Yankee yelled.

Yankee charged after Lefty. He ran outside.

Lefty was waiting for him. He pushed Yankee into a car. Napoleon Cross, the owner of the Cubs, sat there. He had Darlin' in his lap!

Cross and Lefty took Yankee to Wrigley Field. They locked Yankee, Darlin', and Screwie in the owner's box. The next day, the last game of the World Series began—without Darlin'.

Yankee felt terrible. The Yankees were going to lose the Series. And it was all his fault.

Chapter 8

Napoleon Cross was in a great mood. He watched Lefty pitch to Babe down on the field.

"So tragic," Cross said, but he was smiling. "It's Babe's last turn at the plate, and he has no magic bat to rely on."

"Don't listen to him, Yank," Screwie said.

The announcer called the game over the speakers. "And here's the pitch . . . a swing and a miss . . . strike three!"

Cross grinned. "I guess that bat's not much use now."

Darlin' glared at him. "I hope you get splinters!"

Cross left them alone in the box.

"So, Yank, what's the plan now?" Screwie asked.

"There is no plan," Yankee said. "It's over! We failed."

"So what? So the Yankees don't win. Is that why you did this?" Screwie asked him.

"I did it to help my dad," Yankee said softly.

"The game's not over, Yankee,"

Screwie said. "Remember what Babe told you? You've got to keep swinging."

Yankee jumped up. "So how are we getting out of here?" he asked.

Screwie had an idea. "The window."

Yankee threw Screwie through the glass window. It broke, and Yankee climbed through, holding Darlin' tight. Screwie bounced down to the field.

Yankee found another way down. He grabbed a banner and used it to swing down to the field. Then he climbed over the wall and ran to the Yankees dugout.

"Babe!" he called. He put Darlin' in Babe Ruth's hands. "Sorry I didn't get her to you in time. It's my fault the Yankees are losing."

Babe laughed. "It's not your fault, kid. Darlin's a great bat, but she's only a bat. We're just in a slump."

The umpire walked up to the Yankees manager. "That's two outs," he said. "Get your batter in the box."

The manager scratched his head. "We can't put Babe up at bat again. Who do we put at the plate?"

Babe grinned. "How about him?" he said, pointing at Yankee.

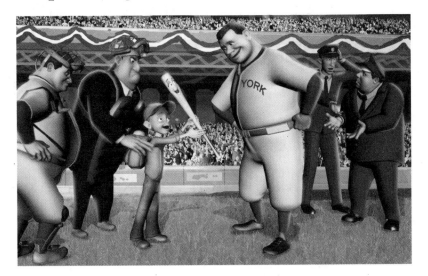

Chapter 9

"But he's just a kid!" the manager said.

"The kid's too short. They'd have to walk him," one player pointed out.

"It just might work," said another player. The manager gave in. Yankee felt like he was in a dream. Babe put Darlin' in his hands. Then he gently pushed Yankee toward home plate.

Screwie rolled up. "You can do it, Yankee! I'll be right here to talk you through it."

But the Cubs catcher picked up Screwie. He tossed him to Lefty on the pitcher's mound.

Yankee was so nervous. He raised Darlin' over his shoulder. He stared at Lefty. Here he was, batting in the World Series! He took a deep breath.

Lefty threw the pitch. It didn't go anywhere near Yankee. But just like he did in the sandlot, Yankee swung at it.

"Strike one!" shouted the umpire.

The catcher threw Screwie back to Lefty. Lefty pitched again. The ball was high and wide, but Yankee swung anyway.

"What are you doing? Don't you remember anything I taught you?" Screwie cried.

Yankee looked around the stadium. One more swing and he would lose the Series for the Yankees. He would fail Babe. He would fail everyone in the stands . . .

Then Yankee saw two people he knew in the stands. His mom and dad!

Yankee suddenly felt calm. He turned back to face Lefty. With his mind clear, he stood the way the Tigers had taught him to. He kept his eye on Screwie, just like Marti had taught him to.

Lefty pitched.

Yankee swung.

"He hit it! The kid hit it!" cried the announcer.

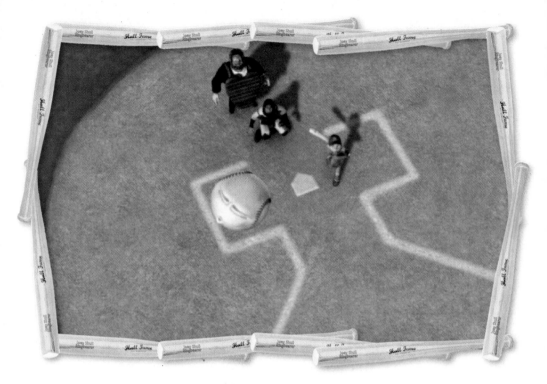

Chapter 10

Yankee hit the ball!

Screwie popped up and fell just below the pitcher's mound. The Cubs weren't expecting that. For a moment nobody knew what to do.

"Run!" Screwie yelled to Yankee.

Yankee took off. He bolted to first base. Lefty ran for Screwie and bumped into the catcher. Lefty picked up Screwie and threw him to first base—but he sailed right past!

Yankee ran for second base, and the players scrambled to get Screwie. They didn't get him in time, so Yankee ran for third.

"Run, Yank! Run!" his dad shouted.

The third baseman dropped Screwie, who rolled into left field. Yankee tagged third base. He had a clear shot for home.

Yankee kept running.

The third baseman threw Screwie to Lefty. Lefty ran

from the pitcher's mound to try to beat Yankee to home plate. He bent down, ready to tag Yankee.

But Yankee ran right over him! He slid into home plate.

"It's a home run! A home run!" the announcer cried. "The Yankees win the World Series!"

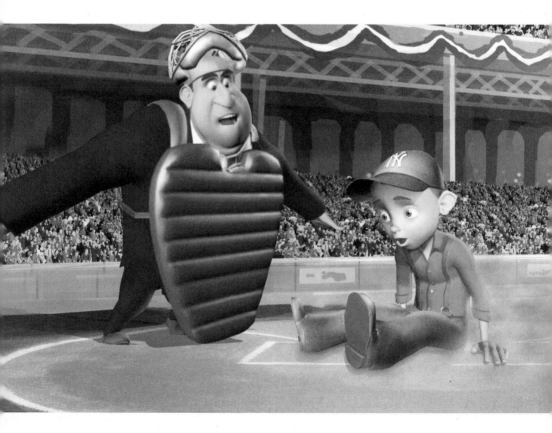

The crowd clapped and cheered. Babe stepped up to thank Yankee. But somebody got to him first.

"Mom! Dad!" Yankee cried.

Yankee's parents hugged him tightly. For Yankee everything else melted away. Babe had his bat, Yankee's father had his job back—and Yankee had hit a home run!

Back in New York, the city held a ticker tape parade for the Yankees. Yankee rode in a car with his parents and Babe—and Darlin' and Screwie, of course.

"It just goes to show you," Screwie said. "You can be the weakest, the smallest, the worst player on the field. People can say you're no good. They can tell you to give it up. And you know what you do? You just keep on swinging!"